Dear Parent:
Your child's love of reading starts here!

Every child learns to read in a different way and at his or her own speed. Some go back and forth between reading levels and read favorite books again and again. Others read through each level in order. You can help your young reader improve and become more confident by encouraging his or her own interests and abilities. From books your child reads with you to the first books he or she reads alone, there are I Can Read Books for every stage of reading:

My First — **SHARED READING**
Basic language, word repetition, and whimsical illustrations, ideal for sharing with your emergent reader

1 — **BEGINNING READING**
Short sentences, familiar words, and simple concepts for children eager to read on their own

2 — **READING WITH HELP**
Engaging stories, longer sentences, and language play for developing readers

3 — **READING ALONE**
Complex plots, challenging vocabulary, and high-interest topics for the independent reader

4 — **ADVANCED READING**
Short paragraphs, chapters, and exciting themes for the perfect bridge to chapter books

I Can Read Books have introduced children to the joy of reading since 1957. Featuring award-winning authors and illustrators and a fabulous cast of beloved characters, I Can Read Books set the standard for beginning readers.

A lifetime of discovery begins with the magical words **"I Can Read!"**

Visit www.icanread.com for information on enriching your child's reading experience.

I Can Read!™ SHARED My First READING

Biscuit Wants to Play

story by ALYSSA SATIN CAPUCILLI
pictures by PAT SCHORIES

SCHOLASTIC INC.
New York Toronto London Auckland Sydney
Mexico City New Delhi Hong Kong Buenos Aires

ISBN-13: 978-0-439-91764-3
ISBN-10: 0-439-91764-6

 Published by Scholastic Inc., 557 Broadway, New York, NY 10012, by arrangement with HarperCollins Children's Books, a division of HarperCollins Publishers.

20 13 14 15/0

Printed in the U.S.A. 40

First Scholastic printing, February 2007

For Peter, Laura, and Billy
with love
—A.S.C.

Woof, woof!
What's in the basket,
Biscuit?

Meow.
It's Daisy!

Meow. Meow.
Daisy has two kittens.

Woof, woof!
Biscuit wants to play
with the kittens.

Meow. Meow.
The kittens want to play
with a leaf.

Woof, woof!

Biscuit wants to play, too.

Woof!

Biscuit sees his ball.

Meow. Meow.

The kittens see a cricket.

Woof, woof!

Biscuit wants to play, too!

Meow. Meow.

The kittens see a butterfly.

Meow. Meow.
The kittens run.

The kittens jump.

Meow! Meow!
The kittens are stuck
in the tree!

Woof!
Biscuit sees
the kittens.

Woof, woof, woof!

Biscuit can help the kittens!

Woof, woof!

Biscuit wants to play
with the kittens.

Meow! Meow!
The kittens want to play
with Biscuit, too!